Produced by Kroha Associates, Inc.
Middletown, Connecticut.

Printed in the United States of America.

ISBN 1-56326-119-7

# Fifi, Come Home

One morning, Fifi ran to her dish to eat her breakfast. But the dish was empty. Minnie had forgotten to feed her. Fifi ran to Minnie's room, where Minnie was hurrying around, picking up toys. When she saw Fifi, Minnie thought she wanted to play.

"Oh, Fifi, I'm sorry, but I can't play with you right now," Minnie said as she patted Fifi's head. "I have to finish my chores so I can meet everyone at Daisy's house. We're going to make plans for the pet show tomorrow. I promise I'll play with you as soon as I get back!"

But Fifi didn't understand. She dropped her toy and ran outside to find her favorite red ball for a game of catch. She picked up the ball in her mouth and ran back to Minnie's room, but now Minnie was getting ready to leave. "I still can't play with you, Fifi," Minnie said as she put on a big red bow. "All my friends are waiting, and I'm late! We'll play catch later!"

    As Minnie hurried out the front door, Fifi pulled her leash off the
doorknob.  She ran outside after Minnie with the leash dangling from
her mouth.

    "I don't have time to take you for a walk right now," Minnie told
Fifi.  "But I will just as soon as I get home."

Minnie picked up Fifi and carried her into the backyard. "Wait here, Fifi," she said as she closed the gate. "When I get back, we'll have some fun! I promise!" Minnie closed the gate and hurried away.

As soon as Minnie was gone, Fifi put her front paws against the gate and pushed. The gate swung open! Minnie was in such a rush, she had forgotten to fasten it! Barking happily, Fifi ran through the gate, across the front yard, and up the sidewalk after Minnie. But Minnie was so far ahead, she didn't notice Fifi was following her!

Fifi ran as fast as she could, but she just couldn't catch up with Minnie.  She saw Minnie crossing a busy street, but before Fifi could follow, the traffic light turned green, and cars went racing past!

When the cars stopped, Fifi dashed across the street, but she couldn't see Minnie anywhere! Fifi ran around a corner. She saw a little girl walking a gray poodle — but no Minnie! Fifi hurried past them. She passed a little boy playing catch in his yard with a huge, shaggy sheep dog. They looked as if they were having a wonderful time. But she didn't see Minnie.

"Here, girl! Here, girl!" Fifi heard someone calling. But it was an old woman on a porch calling to a long, skinny dog to come and eat. Fifi ran up and down one street after another, getting more confused and lost. Everywhere, she saw happy dogs with their human friends. Soon, Fifi was tired. She was hungry and thirsty and sad, and she missed her Minnie more and more.

Meanwhile, Minnie had arrived at Daisy's house. Penny, Lilly, and Clarabelle were already there, talking excitedly about the pet show.

"We're all thinking about what to do with our pets for the show!" Daisy explained. "I'm going to buy my cat Trixie a shiny new ribbon!"

"I'm going to brush my hamster, Cuddles, until his fur shines!" Clarabelle added.

"I got a new cage for Max, my parakeet!" Lilly exclaimed.

"And I'm going to decorate my fish tank with sparkly rocks and maybe even a pretty plant," Penny said.

"We'd all better get ready," Minnie said. "I think I'll go home and give Fifi a bath right now! See you all tomorrow!"

Minnie hurried home. But when she got there, the gate was open, and Fifi wasn't in the backyard. Minnie looked all over the yard and in the house. "Fifi, Fifi, I'm home!" she called, but Fifi didn't come running to greet Minnie with her usual cheery bark.

Minnie was worried. She rushed to the phone and called Daisy. "Oh, Daisy, I can't find Fifi anywhere!" she cried.

"I'll call everyone and ask them to go over and help you look for her," Daisy said. "Don't worry, Minnie. We'll find Fifi."

Soon, Daisy, Penny, Clarabelle, and Lilly were helping Minnie look for Fifi. Lilly and Clarabelle walked up and down the street, calling for Fifi and looking under all the bushes. Penny made signs that read "Lost dog. Reward!" with Minnie's phone number at the bottom. She taped the signs on every telephone pole in the neighborhood. Daisy and Minnie knocked at the neighbors' doors. "Have you seen Fifi?" Minnie asked. But no one had.

Minnie and her friends looked until it began to get dark. One by one, the streetlamps flickered on. "I'm sorry, Minnie," Daisy said at last, "but it's late and I have to go home now."

"Me, too," the others agreed.

During dinner, Minnie could hardly eat. She just moved her food around on her plate and thought about Fifi being cold and hungry. *Oh, Fifi, where are you?* she thought. *Please come home!*

At bedtime, Minnie tossed and turned. She lay awake for a long time, hoping she would soon hear Fifi scratching at the door. She remembered all the wonderful times she and Fifi had shared together. She thought of Fifi wagging her tail, running for her red ball, splashing in the sprinkler, and trotting along on her leash.

Early the next morning, Minnie's friends came by on their way to the pet show.

"Did you find Fifi?" they all asked.

"No," Minnie said sadly. "You'll have to go to the pet show without me. I'm going to keep looking for Fifi. I couldn't think of going to the show without her."

Just as Minnie was leaving to start her search for Fifi, the phone rang.

"I'm calling from the local animal shelter," a lady's friendly voice said. "Someone brought in a very hungry and lonely dog late last night, and she's here safe and sound waiting for you to come and get her!"

"Oh, thank you, thank you!" Minnie exclaimed. "I'm on my way!"

When Minnie got to the animal shelter, Fifi ran to greet her. She was so glad to see Minnie, she jumped into her arms and licked her face all over.

"Oh, Fifi, I'm glad to see you, too!" Minnie cried, hugging Fifi tight.

"It's a good thing Fifi had her collar and tags on," the animal shelter helper said. "Otherwise we wouldn't have known whom to call."

Minnie took Fifi home and fed her a great big breakfast. Then she filled a tub with sudsy water, and gave Fifi a warm bath. Fifi was so glad to be home, she didn't even mind getting wet. When Fifi was dry and fluffy, Minnie tied a red polka-dotted ribbon around her dog's neck and popped her into a wicker basket.

"Come on, Fifi," she said. "If we hurry, we still might be in time for the pet show!"

At the pet show, Penny, Clarabelle, Daisy, and Lilly were sitting glumly beside their pets.

"I suppose I should be glad Trixie won a ribbon for Cutest Cat," Daisy sighed. "But I can't help feeling sad about Fifi being lost."

"It would be a lot more fun to have this award for Best-Decorated Fish Tank if Minnie and Fifi were here, too," Penny agreed.

"I know," Clarabelle said as she held Cuddles. "I can't enjoy Cuddles getting a prize for Softest Fur, when Minnie is so unhappy."

Lilly gave Max an extra pinch of birdseed. "I'm glad Max got an award for Loudest Parakeet, but I wish Fifi were here for him to squawk at."

Just then, Minnie rushed in with Fifi! Daisy, Clarabelle, Penny, and Lilly ran up to her.

"Oh, Minnie, you found Fifi!" Daisy exclaimed. "I'm so happy!"

"Me, too," all of Minnie's friends chimed in.

"But Minnie, you're too late for the show," Clarabelle said. "All the prizes have been given out."

Minnie looked at her friends' pets and all the blue and red ribbons they'd won. Then she looked at Fifi and smiled a smile that seemed to go clear down to her toes.

"It doesn't matter that Fifi didn't win a prize!" Minnie said. "I've still got the best reward of all — and that's my Fifi back with me again!"

I'm so glad to have Fifi back again! From now on, I'll always take especially good care of her.